TEA OVER TALES

THE WORLD OF TABULA RASA

Katie McInnes

Tea Over Tales

Tellwell Talent
www.tellwell.ca

ISBN
978-0-2288-3127-3 (Hardcover)
978-0-2288-3126-6 (Paperback)

Your dreams can never be too big,
your heart can never be too grateful
and your strengths will forever be perfectly unique.

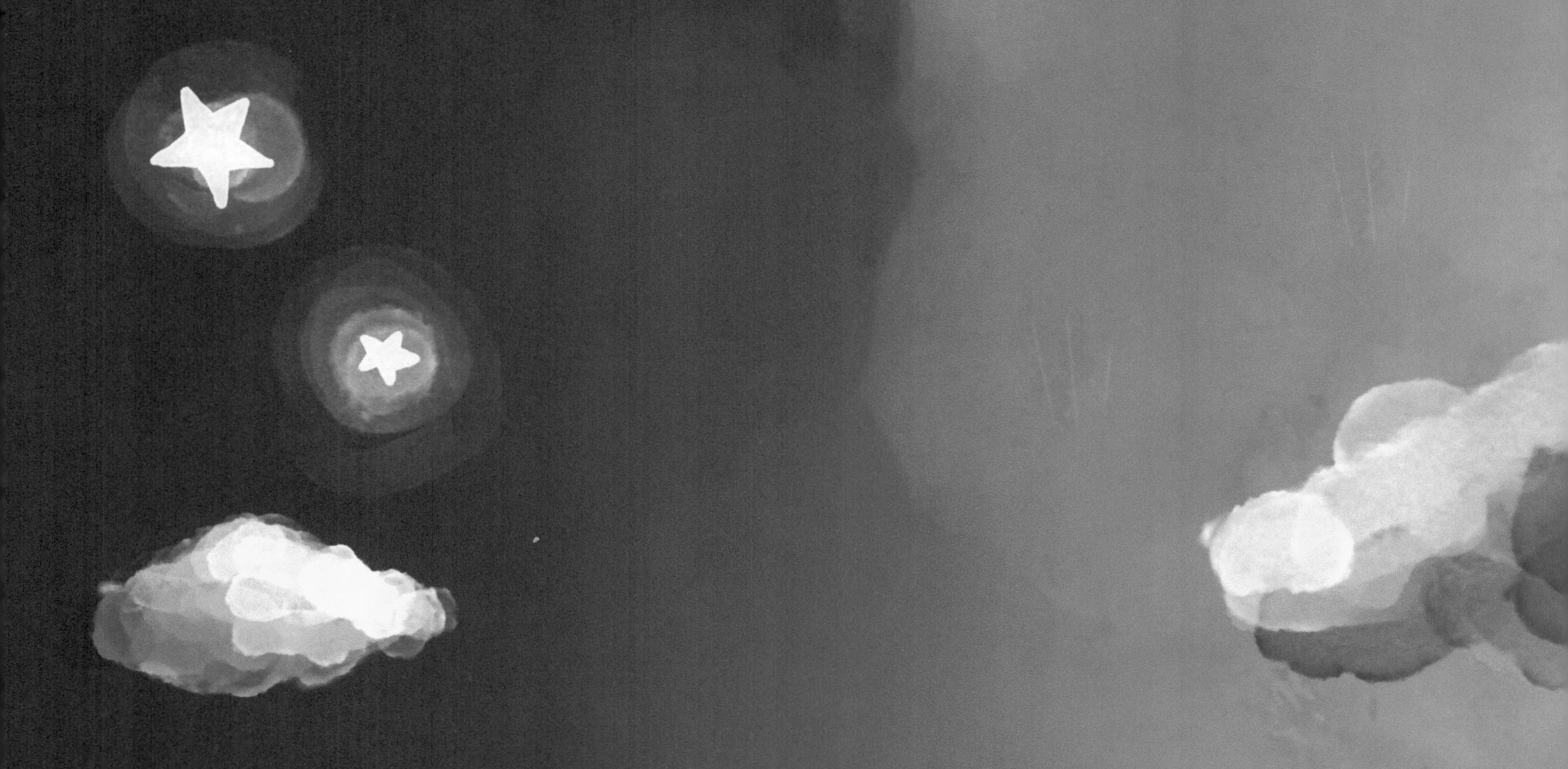

Another day has come and gone,
And Mommy holds me close.
It's storytime as the sun goes down.
I love this time the most.

I say my prayers, turn off the light,
And Mommy tucks me in.

My dolly and I get ready.
Our adventure's about to begin.

I close my eyes and squeeze her tight.
We'll soon be on our way
To the world of Tabula Rasa.
We'll be back when the sun makes
it day.

The world of Tabula Rasa
Is completely made by me.
Each time I close my eyes at night,
It comes out differently.

At first, Tabula Rasa
Is not a fancy site.
There are miles of plain and years of dark
And skies of black and white.

But each step I make, each breath I take,
I create what's true. I begin to fill my world.
You can do *it* too!

Every creature I imagine
Comes floating on a star.

Some with horns and some with fins,
Some are so bizarre.

As I run and dance and sing,
Tabula Rasa comes to life.
Rain falls like prayers from heaven
And oceans turn to ice.

Here in Tabula Rasa, We only think what's kind.

We learn from what is different. We leave no one behind.

The beating of our hearts
Is Mother Nature's guide.
She will offer plenty
If we too will provide

It is here in Tabula Rasa,
We sense the patience of our planet.

No time of any kind,
Just moments we don't take for granted.

In a world of morals and manners,
Where lambs are loyal and
cows say more than moo,

It's important to remember
To love what's true for you.

The wind blows in all directions,

Causing us to change.

But the farther we go.

We become one and the same.

As I fly above my world,
My dolly at my side,
We take in all the sites below.
What an amazing ride!

I can see across the horizon.
The sun has sealed my fate.
See you again tomorrow night,
When I'm ready to create.

The world of Tabula Rasa

Slowly fades to grey.

We wave and shout goodbye
to our friends from far away.

My eyes begin to open.
I'm ready for a brand-new day.
I'll tell Mommy of my adventure.

Oh the things I can say.

CPSIA information can be obtained
at www.ICGtesting.com
Printed in the USA
LVHW070817290521
688874LV00007B/504
* 9 7 8 0 2 2 8 8 3 1 2 7 3 *